For Tom, David and Matthew
M.W.

For Sam
J.W.

First published 1986 by
Walker Books Ltd
184-192 Drummond Street
London NW1 3HP

Text © 1986 Martin Waddell
Illustrations © 1986 Joseph Wright

First printed 1986
Printed and bound by
L.E.G.O., Vicenza, Italy

British Library Cataloguing in Publication Data
Waddell, Martin
Little Dracula's Christmas.—
(The Little Dracula books)
I. Title II. Wright, Joseph
428.6 PE1119

ISBN 0-7445-0686-7
ISBN 0-7445-0544-5 Pbk

Little Dracula's Christmas

Written by

Martin Waddell

Illustrated by

Joseph Wright

WALKER BOOKS
LONDON

It was Christmas Day at the castle, and as the sun went down the Draculas woke up.

'It's Christmas!' cried Little Dracula, biting open his stocking.
'Ga!' said Millicent.

'I wonder if Santa's been,' said Mrs Dracula.
'I wonder if he got his *surprise*,' said Big Dracula,
licking his lips.
They all went down to the Christmas room to see.

'Did we catch Santa?' asked Big Dracula.
'No, Dad,' said Little Dracula.

'Never mind,' said Mrs Dracula, and she gave Big Dracula his presents.

'These presents are for you, Mum,' said Little Dracula.
'The werewolf is from me,' said Big Dracula.

'Presents for Igor!' said Mrs Dracula, and Igor opened them.

'And presents for Millicent!' said Big Dracula.
'What about me?' said Little Dracula.
'Your turn comes next,' said Big Dracula.

'Ooooh!' said Little Dracula.

They all played with their presents.

'Look at me!' cried Little Dracula.
'I can fly like a bat.'

And he flew…

And he landed.

Mrs Dracula was very cross with Little Dracula
and Little Dracula was very sad.
'Cheer up, Little D,' said Big Dracula.
Then Igor said, 'I spy with my little eye...'

'Let's get him!' said Big Dracula.

'Never mind, Dad,' said Little Dracula.
They all went home for their Christmas dinner.

After dinner they watched home movies.

Then Little Dracula and Millicent went to bed.

'Mum!' said Little Dracula. 'You know that Santa
we chased? It was *him*, Mum, it really was! The
real one. The *real* Santa.'
'Yes, dear, of course it was,' said Mrs Dracula.

Mrs Dracula kissed Little Dracula and Millicent
good night.

'It *was* Santa, and we'll catch him next year!'
said Little Dracula, and he went to sleep dreaming
about it.